By

Peter Patrick

&

William Thomas

Agent Time Spy (Book 1)

William Thomas
Peter Patrick

For Ethan, Chelsea, and Sophie

AGENT TIME SPY
BOOK 1

Peter Patrick
William Thomas

CHAPTER 1

I'm the son of a Time Spy.

I know, I know. The son of a Time Spy?! That must be so awesome! You're so lucky! That must be so cool!

But it was totally not.

It was actually *really* boring.

All I ever did was listen to my Time Spy dad talk about the boring adventures he went on. Yesterday, he went back to the dinosaur era and picked a leaf off a tree. A leaf! Are you serious?! He could've tried to solve the dilemmas of time and space, but no. He was more interested in a tiny, little leaf for his leaf collection. Ugh. Boring.

Despite my dad's boring adventures, I still wanted to become a Time Spy one day.

I had completed some of the training, but it was a lot of hard work. To become a Time Spy, a student must complete twenty years of training before the TTSA, that's the Time Traveling Spy Agency, would let you travel forward in time. Twenty years of training! And to go backward in time, a student must complete another ten years of training!

Aw, man. That was so long away! I couldn't even keep focused long enough for my math test next week.

My name is Jetterson Jeffery John James Joseph Baguette, but most people just called me Jett. I'm in the sixth grade, and I loved playing soccer, playing on my computer, and doing anything that involved throwing things.

Even things that shouldn't be thrown. Like pies. I liked throwing pies at people.

This is me.

I wasn't popular at school, but I had my two best friends, Tim and Bella.

This is Tim.

Tim's dress sense was terrible. He dressed like an old man, and the worst thing was, it was his choice.

Once, he walked into a nursing home to see his great-great-great uncle's sister's nephew, but the staff wouldn't let him leave. They thought he belonged there. I had to go into the nursing home and explain that Tim dresses like an old man by choice, but they took a lot of convincing. Eventually, they let him go.

And this is Bella.

Bella was totally cool.

She knew how to skateboard, surfboard, snowboard, bodyboard, and picture-board.

She was so talented. She recently won the school trophy for the person who could walk for the longest time on two hands, while balancing a fruit bowl on their head. It was called the 'Fruit Bowl Two Handed Walk Trophy.' It was the biggest trophy of the year at our school, and they had the 1976 Fruit Bowl Two Handed Walk Champion present the trophy to her. Yep, we had some weird competitions at school.

My home was only five minutes walk from school but I often took longer because there were so many things to be distracted by. Between my home and the school there was a pond, a playground, a park, an arcade, and a small zoo that housed five ants. It wasn't a very interesting zoo.

"Hey, did you hear about Mr. I. Hurtu's wig?" Tim asked as we were walking home after class.

Mr. I. Hurtu was our school principal, and he enjoyed hurting things. In fact, he enjoyed hurting things so much that he held the world record for hurting the most flies in one hour: 5,585. He was quite proud of that record.

"What happened to Mr. I. Hurtu's wig?" Bella questioned.

"It was stolen! Somebody stole his wig!"

"What? Who would be brave enough to steal Mr. I Hurtu's wig?" I said as we walked past the ant zoo. "That person must be totally crazy!"

"It happened just now. And Mr. I. Hurtu looks really angry! He's running around chasing all the flies."

"So now isn't the time to tell him that I accidentally ate his lunch, and then threw his lunchbox in the lake?"

"Um, nope," Tim shook his head. "I don't think you should ever tell him that."

"And did you hear about Mrs. Pet's pet kangaroo?" Bella asked.

"No? What happened to Mrs. Pet's pet kangaroo?"

"It's missing too!" Bella said. "Someone has stolen her kangaroo!"

"What? Who would want to steal a kangaroo?" I asked. "What good would that be?"

"I don't know, but it's very strange," Bella said. "It sounds like someone is stealing things and collecting them. Maybe for some large collection of stolen items?"

"Who would want to collect all those things?"

"Someone that loves collecting, I suppose," Bella replied. "It would have to be a large collection."

"And Mr. Chicken's cow was stolen yesterday!" Tim added. "So many things are going missing."

This was all very weird.

"Hey, what do you get when you cross a Kangaroo with a cow?" I started to laugh at my own joke.

"I don't want to know the answer," Bella replied. "Please don't tell me the answer to your joke. I told you yesterday; I do not want to hear any more of your jokes. Stop."

I don't think Bella liked my jokes.

"A kanga-moo! Hahahaha!" I laughed. "Get it? A Kangaroo and a cow, because cows say 'Moo!' Hahaha!"

Tim and Bella didn't laugh.

They just didn't know good comedy when they heard it.

I told them my awesome jokes all the time, but they never laughed. One day my jokes will make someone laugh. Someone will appreciate my comedic talents one day.

"That's strange," I stopped laughing when I noticed the front door of my house was missing. "Where has the front door to my house gone?"

"It looks like somebody stole it," Bella added.

"Hey Mom, where's the front door?" I asked Mom as I walked into my house. "Why did you take it off?"

"I didn't take it off, Jett! Somebody stole it! Someone stole our front door! But that's not all—my favorite apron is also gone! That's my lasagna apron, Jett! My lasagna apron! I can't cook lasagna without that apron!"

"Why can't you just use another apron?" Tim asked.

"Because that apron has the secret family recipe written on it. I can't cook my secret family lasagna without that apron! I need that apron!"

"What?! Oh no! Who would steal that apron?!" I shouted. "Not the lasagna apron!"

"Only someone who knows about the taste of our family lasagna! I can't cook our family lasagna without that apron!"

No lasagna?!

This was a problem.

This was a massive problem.

I needed to find out what was happening!

CHAPTER 2

Tim, Bella and I ran into Dad's garage where we found him working hard. When he's not working as a Time Spy, he was in there working hard on his latest inventions.

While most garage's are full of cars, bikes, and tools, Dad's garage was more like a workshop for a crazy scientist. It was big—it would fit at least four cars—and the ceiling was high enough for a giraffe to walk in without ducking. There were all sorts of chemicals on one wall, a whiteboard full of mathematic equations on the back wall, and rows and rows of crazy inventions on the shelves.

There was so much stuff in there that Mom complained that she didn't have anywhere to park the car!

"What's that, Dad?"

"This is my new device!" he exclaimed. "I'm so proud of it. It took me so long to make! I had to figure out the dynamics of the device and multiply the multiple options by the number of multiplex choices available for multiplication. That enabled me to multiply the result by the second multiplication of the available angles. And this is the result!"

"What does it do?"

"It's a device that sits on your head to prevent the sun getting into your eyes, or burning your nose. It took me so long to figure this out. I have spent the past week trying to match the perfect design for this great invention. This will change the world, Jett. This will change the world."

"It looks like a hat," Tim said.

"A hat?"

"Yeah. A hat. You know, a hat," I replied to Dad. "Sits on top of your head, stops your nose from getting sunburnt…"

"A hat. Yes… hmmm…"

"You know, things that you can buy from the mall that might look stylish as well? You can get small ones, big ones, round ones, and square ones," Bella mentioned as she started drawing a smiley face on the whiteboard. "You can buy many different colors as well."

"Oh," Dad looked disappointed. "Right. Of course. A hat. All I've done is redesign a hat. Oops. Ok. Don't worry about my new invention."

"Do you have any other new inventions?" I asked. I didn't want Dad to feel bad.

He walked over to the shelves on the left, and rubbed his chin. He stared at the middle shelf, filled with lots of shoes. He had running shoes, clown shoes, and work shoes. They were all stacked on top of each other, piled up in rows of left foot shoes and right foot shoes.

"I've been working on something else anyway. Something way more impressive. I'm sure that my next invention will change the way the world works. It's going to be huge. I'm already halfway through the design process. It's a piece of rubber that goes onto your foot so you don't get spiked by rocks when you walk outside! It's like a glove for your foot! It's so brilliant."

"Um, ok," I shrugged. I didn't want to burst his bubble. "That doesn't sound like a shoe. I'm sure it is a new invention, Dad."

My father was very, very clever, but sometimes he was also very, very dumb.

He also has very, very bad hearing.

And a very, very big little toe.

Sometimes, I wonder how he solves anything!

Dad works as the head Time Spy in the Time Traveling Spy Agency, the TTSA. The agency was developed by people of the past, present, and future to ensure that Time Travelers don't break the rules of time travel.

There are very strict rules for traveling through time. If traveling backward in time, then a person must not disturb anything that could alter the fabric of history. Once, Dad went back 4,000 years to collect another leaf for his leaf collection, and he accidently landed the time machine on a unicorn. That wouldn't have been so bad, but it was the first ever unicorn born.

That's why there aren't any unicorns in the world today.

There are only four people that are allowed to use a time machine, and they've been training for an extremely long time. There's my dad, and three other Time Spies—Dr. Jo King from England, Dr. Harry Back from Russia, and Professor Tim. E. Traveler from China.

The TTSA is super important.

The agency governs the rules of time travel and monitors the realm of time to ensure that those rules are not broken. They have machines and technology from the future that enable them to track whoever is traveling through time, and stop them from possibly destroying time itself.

There was a group of rebel time travelers from the future that continued to travel backward in time, breaking the rules of time travel, and threatening the very existence of reality. It was the agency's job to capture them and lock them away.

"Dad, all these inventions are super cool but we have a problem," I said. "There are some very strange things happening and we need to know what's causing it. That's why we came to you."

"That sounds serious. What's the problem, Jett?"

"Lots of things are being stolen from all over the town. First, it was Mr. I. Hurtu's wig, then Mrs. Koala's kangaroo, then Mr. Chicken's pet cow, then the front door of our house…"

"Hmm… that does sound like a problem, Jett. How will someone knock on our door if there's no front door?"

"Well, all that wouldn't be so bad, but Mom's apron has also been stolen."

"No!" Dad screamed in terror. "Not her lasagna apron?!"

"Yes, Dad. Her lasagna apron."

"Oh no!" Dad started crying. "That means no more lasagna! This is a disaster, Jett! A disaster!"

"It's a problem, Dad. It's a real big problem."

"We have to solve this…" Dad composed himself, and scratched his head for a few moments. Then he stroked his chin. Then he started running his finger over the tip of his nose. I have no idea why he does that. "This is an interesting development, Jett. It might be a coincidence, but over the past two days, we've had a lot of abnormal movement on the Time Traveler Radar. It's been unusual movement that we can't explain."

"What's the Time Traveler Radar?" Tim asked. "It sounds like a radar that tells people if there has been any movement through space and time."

"No, Tim, it's a lot more complicated than that. It's a radar that tells us if there has been any movement through time and space. If anyone travels through the realms of time, then it shows up on our radar." Dad walked to the end of the garage and pulled a poster off the wall. Behind the poster was a really cool radar. It looked brand new. "In fact, a recent traveler has traveled to our time, and then left again. The traveler has done this numerous times over the past two days. We have been trying to locate the position of his time machine landing, however we cannot pinpoint the exact location yet. We're close, but we haven't been able to find it. He's too quick."

"Do you think it's related to the stolen objects?" Bella looked over my father's shoulder at the radar. "Maybe a time traveler is stealing the items to take home?"

"It could be, but I'm not sure, Bella. We've had suspicions that someone is traveling through the realms of time and collecting numerous items. The person then returns to the future to sell those items as perfect antiques," Dad replied. I'm not sure he hears anything that we're saying. "However, they're not really antiques; they're merely items stolen from the past to sell in the future."

"Sounds like a good business idea to me," Bella said.

"Look!" Dad shouted, pointing to a large spike in his radar monitoring system. "Look at that signal!"

We stood around the radar at the side of the room, staring at the screen. There was a long wavy line on the screen, and occasionally it beeped.

"What is it?"

"Someone is traveling through time right now! It's happening now. I've got to go and investigate!"

CHAPTER 3

After Dad ran off to try and find out who was traveling through time without permission from the TTSA, Tim and Bella decided to go home. I suggested that we go search for the missing items, but they both had excuses. Bella said she had to practice her finger dancing moves—cool, right? —and Tim said he had science homework to complete, which was not so cool.

I couldn't finger dance very well, it looked like I was just tapping on the table, and I didn't feel like working on my homework, so I went into the kitchen for a bite to eat. Mom was in the living room, trying to remember the recipe to her lasagna but she was really struggling to remember all the 155 ingredients. It really was a complex recipe.

I went into the kitchen and made a sandwich—two slices of bread, five pieces of chocolate, five crisps and five pieces of popcorn. I called it my 'Five-Alive' sandwich. Delicious. I was just about to bite into the Five-Alive when Bella called my phone.

"Quick, Jett! You have to come to my house! This is an emergency!" she screamed. "It's terrible!"

Putting down my sandwich, I ran out the door, down the street, past the zoo with five ants, and around another corner to Bella's house. When I arrived, she was standing in her front yard, looking very worried. There was a large pig pen in her yard, but nothing inside. I didn't know she had a pig.

Bella's house was nice—it was a two-story white house with a large yard. The grass was perfectly cut, the flowers were all growing in rows, and she had fifteen large cactus plants lining the fence. I know why she didn't like to play near the fence.

"Bella," I said, still puffing after the run. "What's the emergency?"

"My pig is missing."

"Your pig?"

"My pig!"

"You have a pig?"

"Yes, Jett, I have a pig. And now my sweet, adorable, cute Chris P. Bacon is missing!"

"That's your pig's name? Chris P. Bacon?"

"Yes. He's named after my grandfather, Chris P. Bacon. My grandfather was a famous pig juggler for the world's greatest circus. He was the best pig juggler in the country. He was known for his famous trick of juggling six pigs at once."

"A pig juggler?"

"Yes, Jett. A pig juggler is a person that juggles pigs. My grandfather was so good that he won the award for pig juggling excellence ten years in a row."

"There's an award for pig juggling excellence?"

"Of course. It's called the 'Award for Pig Juggling Excellence.'"

"Right." I scratched my head, looking at the empty pig pen. "How big was your pig?"

"He was so cute," Bella said as she showed me a picture of her standing next to her pet pig. "Chris P. Bacon was such a sweety."

"Whoa. That's a big pig," I said as I looked at the photo of Bella and her pet pig. "It's the size of a horse."

"That's my little, cute, adorable pet."

"So what happened to it? Pigs that size don't just wander off without anybody noticing it. Actually, pigs that size don't do anything without somebody noticing."

"Chris P. Bacon was here this morning, and I made sure that I locked his pig pen. There's no way he could have just walked away. That's why it's really strange that my poor little piggy is missing. Somebody must have stolen it! Somebody took my pig!"

Bella was worried. I could see the tears in her eyes. She must've really loved that pig.

"Why would anybody steal a pig?" I asked. "Are you sure that he was stolen?"

"Yes! There's no other way he could have gotten out of—"

"Help!" Tim shouted as he came charging into Bella's yard. "Help me! Somebody help me!"

"What's wrong!?"

"My favorite history book has been stolen! My favorite history book, Jett! This is a disaster! It's my favorite history book! Someone has stolen my favorite history book!"

Tim really liked history.

In fact, he liked history so much that sometimes he pretended that he lived in the past. Just yesterday, I found him walking around his yard pretending he was riding a dinosaur.

"What on earth is going on?" I questioned. "Things are going missing all over the city, and it doesn't make sense. A normal thief would rob a bank, or a jewelry store, or steal something valuable. But this thief is stealing all sorts of random things. I don't think we're dealing with a normal thief here. I think we're dealing with something a lot more sinister. There must be something more to this."

"Let's think about where things are going missing," Bella said. "We might be able to establish a pattern of behavior if we track where things are being stolen from."

We walked past the cactus plants, careful not to get spiked, and into Bella's home. She went to the draws in her kitchen and pulled out a map of our town. I grabbed a red pen and put dots where items had been stolen from.

"The principal's wig was stolen at school, the kangaroo here, the cow there, the pig from Bella's house, the apron from my house, and Tim's history book from his house."

We studied the map and realized that it was almost a perfect circle.

"It looks like the thief is stealing things within a few miles of where he must be hiding," Tim said. "So what's in the middle of the circle?"

"That's Dark Park."

"Dark Park?" Tim shook as he said the name. "You mean the scary park where nobody goes?"

"That's the one," Bella said softly. "*The* Dark Park."

"Then that's where we should go!" I said. "If we're going to solve this crime then that's where we need to look! I bet our criminal, along with all the stolen goods, is right in the middle of that park. We have to go there!"

"No way," Bella said. "I'm not going there. Lot's of bad things happen in Dark Park."

"Uh-uh," Tim said. "Nope. Me neither. There's no way that we should go there. Have you heard the stories about that park? They say that anyone who enters Dark Park never returns the same. They see things that change them forever. I don't want to see things, Jett. I don't want to change. I'm happy the way I am."

"Of course we're going there!" I said, and started to walk out the door. "We have to find my Mom's lasagna apron!"

CHAPTER 4

As the name suggested, Dark Park was dark. Even in the middle of a sunny summer's day, the park was dark.

And windy.

And cold.

And very scary.

It was a totally bizarre place. It was in the middle of our town but it was always empty. Nobody ever went in there. Even the gardeners refused to work on the gardens, but somehow the gardens were always perfectly maintained. I heard a rumor that a ghost gardener worked on mowing the lawns and trimming the trees every night. I didn't know if that was true, but I didn't want to find out either.

Reluctantly, Tim and Bella followed me to Dark Park. They didn't want to come, they didn't want to go near Dark Park, but they really wanted to find their stolen goods. We had no other choice.

As we walked up to the old iron gates that led into the park, the noise of the creaky fence sent a shiver up my spine. There were old leaf-less trees that looked like they were from a horror movie, bushes that looked like people were hiding behind them, and every stone looked like it was from a graveyard.

A large dark cloud sat overhead, and as soon as we stepped into the park, the temperature dropped, and it looked like it was dark enough to be the middle of the night.

Tim and Bella walked behind me as we entered, and I could hear Tim's teeth chattering.

If there were a competition for the eeriest, gloomiest, nastiest park in the world, this place would win every time.

In fact, this place would be first in the Hall of Fame for the World's Creepiest Parks.

After we entered the park, we walked through the wind and cold for five minutes before we saw something behind a tree. It was so dark that we had to squint just to see anything.

The wind whistled past us, and I think I heard someone whispering. I'm sure I even saw a set of glowing eyes in one of the bushes.

"Look at that," Tim whispered while holding onto my arm. "It's Mr. I. Hurtu's wig."

"We're in the right place," I murmured. "This must be where the thief is hiding. This must be the place where he's bringing all the stolen goods."

"Good. Problem solved. We've done it. Let's go home," Tim said. "There's nothing more we can do today. We'll tell Mr. I. Hurtu his wig is here, and we'll just leave it at that. He can tell the police. We should go now. Let the professionals handle it."

"No, Tim," I replied. "We can't leave now. We have to find out what's happening. We can't just walk away. We have to find all the other stolen goods. And there's no way that I'm leaving here without my Mom's apron. I can't live a lasagna-less life."

We were squinting, looking for any of the other stolen objects when suddenly, a bright light began to glow in front of us.

"Whoa!"

"What's that?" Bella asked.

"Shhh…." I said. "Quick. Hide."

We jumped behind a nearby rock, hiding from the bright glow.

The light swirled, spun and sparkled. A whirling noise began, and the best I could figure, it was coming from where the light was shining.

I peered out from behind the rock, desperate to see what was causing the light.

Then, out of nowhere, a machine appeared!

Like completely out of nowhere! It wasn't there a minute ago!

It looked like a small rocket, only big enough for one person, but the top was completely made out of glass. There was a control panel in the front, and four little stands for the machine to rest on.

And out of that machine, a man came out!

It was a strange looking machine, but an even stranger looking man!

"Who's that?" Bella whispered. "And what's he doing?"

"I don't know. We should ask him. He looks friendly."

"Um… no, he doesn't. He looks evil," Tim said, but it was too late. I had already stood up, and the bizarrely dressed man was looking straight at me. "Jett!"

"Excuse me, who are you?" I asked, stepping forward. "I'm asking because we're trying to locate a thief, and it appears that you've landed in the exact spot where the thief should be. Do you know anything about all the stolen goods around here?"

"Go away, little child," he stated. "I'm a very busy man and I have no time to talk with you. Go back to school."

The weirdly dressed man turned and started walking away.

"Hey! Mr. I'm-too-cool-to-wear-normal-clothes, I asked you a question!" I shouted. "You should answer it!"

Slowly, he turned around and… **ZAP!**

He shot me with some type of zapper ray gun!

And the electric force sent me flying!

Ouch!

It hurt! Who would've thought that an electric zapper actually hurt?!

I landed in the bushes and felt dazed by the shot. By the time Bella and Tim had reached me, the man was already gone. He really didn't want to talk.

"Jett! Talk to me, Jett! Are you ok?" Bella asked. "Jett?"

"I'm fine. I'm fine. Just a little sore," I shook my head. "That was quite a shock."

"Who was that?"

"I have no idea. But I think you're right, Tim. I don't think he's friendly," I said. "Friends don't shoot each other with zapper ray guns."

"How do you know what sort of gun that was?" Tim asked. "I've never seen anything like that!"

"I've seen my dad use one like that before. It's a zapper ray gun from the future."

"You mean the outlandishly dressed man is from the future?" Bella asked. "And that ray gun is also from the future?"

"He must be. He must be the one that Dad was talking about! He must be traveling through time and stealing all our things! That's why all the things are going missing! We've found the thief!"

"Shhh…" Tim said. "He's coming back."

We hid behind another rock and watched the man go into a bush.

That's where I saw a set of eyes staring at us earlier. A cold wind blew around the park, and then I heard the whispering again. I kept my eyes on the large bush, but it was hard to see what was happening.

When the man walked out of the bush, he was carrying Bella's pig!

"Chris P. Bacon! My pig!" Bella leapt up. "That's my pig!"

"Quiet." Tim grabbed Bella's arm to stop her going any further. "We don't want him to zap us. Remember, he's not a friendly guy."

We watched the weird man squeezed the pig into the machine, and then he climbed in himself. I don't think he expected the pig to be so big.

"What's he doing with my pet pig?" Bella asked. "Where's he taking him?"

"I'm not sure, but we should stop him from leaving." I leapt up and ran towards the machine. "Oi! Stop!"

But then...

The machine disappeared! Into thin air!

"No!" Bella yelled. "My pig! The stupidly dressed man stole my pet! They've gone!"

"It's ok, Bella. We'll sort this out," I tried to calm Bella down. "We'll find a way to get your pet pig back. We have to."

"But what if we never see him again? What if my pet pig is gone forever?"

"Hmmm…" I tried to think about it for a few moments, rubbing my chin and making weird movements with my eyebrows. Then I snapped my fingers. "I've got it! All we have to do is travel to the future, grab our stuff, and return. Easy."

"So my pig is in the future?"

"Yep. Chris P. Bacon is now a future pig."

"But how will we get to the future?"

"I'll call my dad. He'll know what to do. Now that we know where the man is, my dad will travel into the future, and get all our things back. He'll help us."

I reached into my back pocket, and pulled out my phone. I had Dad's number on speed dial.

"Dad!"

"Yes, Jett," Dad answered the phone. "It's lovely to talk with you. Thank you for calling."

"Dad, there was a man-"

"A van?"

"No, Dad—a man."

"A can?"

"No! A man!"

"A pan? What are you talking about, Jett? What pan?"

"No, Dad! I said 'there was a man!'"

"Ok, Jett. That's nice. There are men all over the city. It's no big deal. In fact, half the population are men. But listen, I'm very busy right now trying to solve the case of a time traveling man. I'm trying to locate him right now. I think we've had some recent travel through time, and it appears that the traveler has landed in our city again. I'm trying to pinpoint his exact location using the Exact Location Radar. We're close to finding him."

"Yes, Dad, there was a man-"

"Sorry son, I can't chat about the van now. I've got to go and find out where this man is."

Then Dad hung up. "Arggh!"

"What are we going to do now?!" Tim asked. "We can't do this ourselves!"

"It looks like this is the spot he keeps coming back to." Bella closed her fist. She looked angry, but then I would be angry if someone stole my pig. "I'm sure that he'll come back here to steal more things from us. If we wait long enough, he'll come back to us."

"So we should all just go home then?" Tim suggested. "Maybe have a nice warm glass of milk and then go to bed? That seems like the best thing to do right now."

"No way." I squinted my eyebrows and clenched my fist as well. "It's up to us to stop this madman!"

CHAPTER 5

As the sun set, Dark Park became creepier and creepier. I'm sure I saw a ghost in the distance.

We waited at the same spot in Dark Park for the machine to return. We waited hours, and hours, and hours…

Tim was too scared to move, and Bella was pacing around in a circle, trying to figure out a way to save her pet pig. I stared at the trees, trying to spot any movements, but when I did see something, I looked away. Even the grass seemed creepy in that park. The smell of the park was scary as well—it smelt like bats mixed with crisps. It made me hungry and scared at the same time.

Tim really wanted to leave, but neither Bella or I were going anywhere, and there was no way that Tim was going to try and run to the gate by himself. He wouldn't make it.

As the park became even darker, Tim and Bella were starting to look really scared, so I began telling them some more of my great jokes. That would take their mind off being frightened.

"Hey Bella, what's the warmest place in the room?"

"I don't want to know." Bella shook her head. "Please don't finish that joke."

"The corner! Because it's always 90 degrees! Get it? 90 degrees! The angle is 90 degrees, and the warmth, and-"

"Stop." Bella held up her hand. "Please stop."

I don't think she liked that joke, but I was sure she would like my next one.

"What did one wall say to the other wall?"

"Please don't tell me the answer."

"I'll meet you at the corner! Haha!" I laughed, but nobody else did. "Get it?"

"We get it." Tim and Bella said at the same time, while they both also rolled their eyes. "We understand the joke."

"Well, what did the fish say when he swam into the wall?"

No one answered. They must've been waiting for my great punchline.

"Dam! Hahahaha!"

I'm so funny.

But I don't think they liked my jokes. They must've been too exhausted.

"Please stop. Just stop," Bella complained. "I don't want to hear another joke."

Just as I was about to tell another one of my awesome jokes…

The light appeared again!

It whirled, it buzzed, and then—pop!

The machine was back!

This time, I didn't mess around.

"Oi!" I shouted out to the guy from the future, as I marched towards the machine. "You and I need to talk!"

As soon as the man stepped out of his machine, he reached for his zapper ray gun again!

"Wait!" I shouted. "Don't shoot me! You have to talk to me! My dad is a member of the Time Traveling Spy Agency, and he'll make sure that you have all sorts of problems if you zap me again! I am not the kid that you want to zap."

"Oh, the TTSA. Yes. I know them." He groaned. "The agency has tried to stop me before. They haven't though. Clearly. Because if they had stopped me, I wouldn't be standing here. But I am standing here. So obviously, I have not been stopped yet. Because I am still here. Not stopped."

"Ok…" I said. "But who are you?"

"I am The Collector!"

"Why do you want all this stuff?"

"I'm called The Collector. I thought that would make it pretty clear to you. It's what I do. I collect things. If I were called The Tickler, you would expect me to tickle things. Or if I were The Winker, you would expect me to wink. If I was the Sprinkler, you'd expect me to water the grass. But I'm not! I'm The Collector! And right now my collection of collected things needs collected items from this year."

"You mean you collect things from all of time?"

"That's right! You're not as stupid as you look! I have dinosaurs, and knights, and cavemen, and phistzings-"

"What's a phistzing?"

"It's from the future. Well, not my future. Your future. It's from the past. But not your past, my past. Which is your future. And not your past."

"But don't you change the future every time you come back?"

"Of course not! There are layers in time that exist parallel to each other, and when you travel between them, the basic parallels of time travel are reversed. So if you travel sideways through the parallels, you're not affecting the future or the past, you're merely drifting between the present time while traveling forward to the past. Of course, when you drift from the past to the future through the parallels of time, you're no longer in the present, but you're in a multi-dimension of parallel lines. So your future or past is not affected by my decision to travel through the parallels of time unless I was to travel directly backward down the parallel of time that I'm currently on. Then that would change the parallels of the future and the past. This is all very easy to understand."

"Uh?" I said.

"Young boy, it's all very simple. Time exists in parallel columns, held together by the forces of time-specific gravitational pull. When the rings of time-specific gravitational pull begin to co-exist between the parallels, it enables a person to travel on the rings through the sub-terrain of the parallel columns. Within these sub-terrains of parallel columns are small holes within the rings of time-specific gravitational pull. Within those small holes, are square diamonds of backward force. These square diamonds of backward force enable the existence of the parallel columns, and thus, allows a person to travel through the parallels of time without affecting the past, or the future, but merely affecting the present!"

"Uh?"

"And not your present, but my present, because time still exists as I travel through the square diamonds of backward force upon the rings of time. So while I go to the past, it's still my present, and even when I go to the future, time is relative to my perception. So in the past or in the future, it's still my present. To access my present then, I would have to travel the exact direction of the gravitational pull that was happening during my existence on those parallel columns."

"What?"

"Never mind, little boy. You'll understand one day. But right now, I'm collecting items for my collection. But my time machine is so small that I can only take one thing at a time. For my next item, I'm going to take this apron back to the future."

"You can't. That's my Mom's apron. I can't let you take that!"

"This isn't just your Mom's apron, young boy! This apron holds the key to the greatest lasagna empire of the future. In the future, your Mom's secret recipe becomes the best selling lasagna recipe of all-time! She starts a lasagna empire that becomes the biggest company in the world! With this apron, I will be able to make a rival lasagna empire and make quad-dillions of dollars!"

"Quad-dillions? That's not even a word!"

"It is in the future!"

"Well, you can't have the apron!"

"You can't stop me!"

"Yes, I will!"

"No, you can't!"

"Yes, I will!"

"Oh, ok." The Collector shrugged his shoulders. "Here you go then."

He went to hand the apron back to me. Well, that was easy.

But just as he handed the apron across…

WHACK!

He hardcore kicked me in the stomach!

Then…

CRASH!

He picked me up and threw me into a tree!

Ouch!

I was in so much pain, but I couldn't let him take that apron!

I climbed back to my feet and began to chase him again!

Just as I was about to grab him…**BANG!**

He knocked me to the ground with a totally futuristic move!

And then he put on my Mom's apron!

"If you live long enough, come and see me in the future. I'll bake you the perfect lasagna, kid," said The Collector.

He walked back to his machine and then disappeared into the future.

Or the past.

Or the present-future.

Or through some parallelogram of time-squirting water hoses.

Yeah. I had no idea where he went.

All I knew was that he was no longer there, and he had my Mom's apron—and I had to get it back!

CHAPTER 6

In a rush, we went to find my dad. He'd know what to do. He was one of the best spies on the entire planet, and he'd know exactly how to solve this. He'd know how to stop The Collector.

As fast as we could, we ran out of Dark Park, down the street, past the zoo, past the arcade, and into my garage. Dad had the door open as he tried to study the readings on his computer.

"Dad!" I yelled as soon as I saw him. "We need—"

"Sorry, son. I can't talk. I'm really busy right now. I'm trying to find the thief. This is a very hard case to work out. There seems to be things missing from all over our city. It's all very peculiar."

"But Dad, we know what's happening! It's a person named The Collector!"

"Hector? Who is Hector?"

"Not Hector! The Collector!"

"The Connector? What are you talking about, Jett?"

"The Collector!"

"The Selector?"

"No, Dad! The-"

"Sorry son, I haven't got time for these games. I have to find the person who is stealing all the things! We'll talk later, and you can tell me a story about the nectar."

"But Dad! I've-"

"Sorry son, I have to go. This is too important."

And then he walked away back to the house!

When he was in a mood like this, there was no talking to him. He could only focus on one thing at a time, and no matter what I said, he wasn't going to listen to it.

Agh!

My dad was no help.

We'd have to get that apron back by ourselves!

I sat in the garage with my friends, thinking over our options. I couldn't let The Collector get away with this, not when Mom's lasagna was at stake. I couldn't imagine a world without Mom's lasagna—what a sad, sad world that would be.

"What are we going to do?" Bella asked. "If you're dad doesn't help us, how are we going to stop him?"

Turning to look at Tim and Bella, I smiled.

"No way," Tim said. He knew what I was going to say next. "Uh-uh. Nope. Not a chance, Jett. We're not doing that."

"My dad won't listen," I told my friends. "He's too busy trying to find the guy that we've already found. We'll have to do this ourselves!"

"Why don't we just give up?" Tim asked. "I can buy another history book. And Bella can buy another pig."

"No way! I need my Mom's apron back. Without that apron, I'll never have Mom's great lasagna again!"

"But what can we do?" Bella asked. "We can't beat him. He's too ninja-y."

"We need a plan."

"Do you have one?"

"I do." I made a steely gaze into the distance. "We have to go back to the machine, go to the future, and steal back the things that were stolen from us! Hold onto your hats, team. This is going to get dangerous…"

CHAPTER 7

We had to go back into Dark Park.

Tim really, really didn't want to go this time—Bella and I had to drag him past the gates. Once inside the park, he wouldn't leave our sides. Half the trees we passed looked dead, and the other half looked like the branches were moving, reaching out as if trying to grab us.

I didn't like this park—I wouldn't come here to play football on the weekend—but we had no choice. We walked back through Dark Park to where the machine had been landing.

Just as we arrived, we heard the whirling noise again. The light appeared in front of us, spinning around and around.

"Time to hide," I said, and we jumped behind a bush. "He's back."

"What are we going to do?" Tim whispered. "Do you have a plan to stop him?"

"As soon as The Collector is back inside the time machine with his next load of stolen goods, we jump onto the outside of the machine. If we hold on tight, the machine will take us to the future, and we can take back our things!"

"Then how do we get back from the future?" Bella asked. "I don't want to be stuck in the future. Who knows what could be happening there?"

"We just steal the machine and fly back. Easy."

"Do you even know how to work a time-traveling machine?"

"If my dad can do it, how hard can it be?"

We ducked down behind a small bush, and watched as The Collector walked through the park and picked up more stolen goods that he stored behind another rock. The light coming from the machine was enough to see around the park, and it was then that we saw all the items that he had stolen.

He walked over to the pile of stolen goods, picked something up, and went back to his machine with more stolen goods. This time he was carrying Benny Banger's drum kit!

As soon as The Collector climbed inside his time machine, he started to work the controls.

Hiding behind the bush, we waited for the perfect time to jump onto the back of the machine. When The Collector locked the door to the machine, we made our move.

"Go!" I shouted. "Move!"

We ran towards the back of the machine and jumped on it!

"Hold on!" I bellowed. "This is going to be rough!"

The machine started to shake and then whirl!

Here we go…

CHAPTER 8

Whoa.

I was feeling totally dizzy after the machine stopped whirling.

That was a really strange experience. We were spun around and around, and then we stopped.

There were lots of colors, like a rainbow, and it seemed like we were going through a small tunnel. We were spinning, trying to hold onto the machine, and then, all of a sudden, we were back in the park.

"Where are we?" Tim asked. "Is this the future?"

I looked around. It looked like the same park. It smelt like the same park.

There was even dog poo right where we had landed on the grass.

It was still dark, the trees were still scary, and the wind still sounded like it was whispering to us. Yep, absolutely, the same park.

"The machine must have spun us off just before we launched. We must still be in the present time. Our plan didn't work."

"Um," Bella said. "Nope. I don't think so. Look!"

We looked to where Bella was pointing, and we saw our town in the distance. Except it was no longer a town, it was now full of sky-rise buildings!

And flying cars!

The buildings were styled in a way I hadn't seen before, and the lights seemed brighter than normal. The weather was warmer too. All the bright lights from the tall buildings highlighted the outside of the park, making it clear that we were no longer in our time.

"Wow. Our plan must have worked. This must be the future!" I said as a small robot dog started doing a poo right in front of me! "And why is a robot dog doing a poo?"

The dog was metal and square, but moved with smooth movement. He even barked a little after he had finished his business.

"Quick," Tim said. "Someone's coming. Hide!"

We hid behind a small bush at the side of a walkway.

Tucked away, we watched as someone walk past. It was The Collector, and he was carrying my front door!

"It's him," I said. "We have to follow him and find out where he's taking all our stuff, but don't let him see us."

"Are you sure that's a good idea?" Tim stayed behind the bush. "Shouldn't we just wait here for a while? Maybe your dad will come here soon. Or maybe we should call the future police, tell them what's happening, and let them sort it out."

"We didn't travel all the way to the future just to see a robot dog do a poo. Although, that was pretty cool." I stood up. "Come on, let's follow him."

Quietly, we followed The Collector out of the park, making sure that he couldn't see us. We hid behind trees, bushes, rocks, and bubbles. Yep, the future has bubbles.

As we followed The Collector, we couldn't help but look at the city. It had changed so much! It was so slick, and clean, and really, really cool. I never thought my city would look that cool. Flying cars were zipping around everywhere, lights were flashing on and off, and even from a distance, we could see that people were weirdly dressed.

"Look at the mall—it's massive! It's got to have five thousand shops in it." Bella pointed to the city. "And the school is huge too!"

"Oh man, they still have school in the future?" I said. "I would've thought that somebody would have invented a pill to educate everyone by now."

"And is that a robot person?" Tim spotted something in the distance, at the edge of the now not-so Dark Park. "They have robots walking around the streets."

"Come on," I said to the others. "I know that the future is cool, but we have a job to do. Let's keep following that thief. We don't want him to get away from us. And there's no time like the present!"

"Except when you aren't in the present," Tim quipped. "Because we're in the future."

We kept following The Collector, and he walked out of the park to the entrance of a super modern house where the ant zoo used to be.

It was an enormous building, around fifteen levels tall, and it was shaped like the letter 'C'. It was smooth and shiny, and it had flying cars driving right past it. I couldn't believe what I was seeing. They sure have some crazy style in the future.

"That must be where he lives," Bella said as we hid behind a tree near the entrance. "Cool house though."

"And it must be where all our stuff is," I said. "We have to get in there to get all our stuff back. But I don't think it'll be easy. It looks like a very futuristic house, and I can only imagine the sort of security that he has in there. We need a plan of attack."

"We should go home to our time, and get your dad. That's the best plan." Tim was biting his fingernails. "We'll leave all the fighting to him. And he can bring all our stuff home from the future for us."

"No way. We can't let this opportunity pass us by. We don't even know what year it is. Let's just wait here until The Collector leaves the house and then sneak in, and get our stuff back. Then we can go home, and get my dad. He can arrest The Collector, but we have to get our stuff back first. We need that apron."

"What about the security system in the house?" Bella was staring at the giant house. "I imagine that it would be ultra-high-tech. If we wait until he leaves, we'll have to break through the security system. And I don't like our chances."

"Tim?" I questioned my friend. "Can you do anything about that security system?"

"I can have a look, if I have to," Tim said. One of the benefits of having the smartest guy in school as your best friend is that he can solve most computer problems.

"Good. Then that's our plan. We'll wait until he leaves the building, and then we'll break in."

Near the entrance to his house, next to a very old sign about the ant zoo, we waited behind a bush.

We waited…

And waited.

And waited.

We waited outside his house for ages…

The future can be quite boring when you're doing nothing!

"Look," Bella said finally. "It's The Collector! He's leaving the house."

The Collector left the building, heading back into the future Dark Park. He must've been going back to his machine to steal more items from our time.

Sneaking up to the entrance of the building, we saw a computer panel next to the front door. It was very complex with lots of buttons, and with lots of letters that I hadn't even seen before.

"Tim, can you hack the security system even if you can't read what it says?"

"I'll do my best." Tim drew a deep breath and started to tap codes into the system. "It seems to be a level six dynamic quad security system. If I can find the hole in the firewall defenses, I can break through the backlines of the quad, and use that against the dynamic four-walls. If I can do that, then the eight-bit understudy can be cracked by using the sideways movements of the administration files. Once we are able to move the administration files sideways, the firewall should open up long enough for us to disengage the number wisp on the sanctuary classification. It's at that point where we can disable the security system. Understand?"

"Um, yep. Totally understand. I understand it all. Totally," I nodded. "If there were an award for the most understanding person on the planet, I would win it. It would be called the 'Jett Baguette Award for Understanding Things.' Yep. I totally understand what you said."

I had no idea what he said.

"Yes!" Tim said as the front door swung open. "I got it."

"You did it!" Bella patted Tim on the back. "You managed to crack a security system in the future. Tim, you're awesome!"

"It's time." I gently pushed the door open. "Time to get our things back!"

CHAPTER 9

The inside of the massive house was very cool.

The hallway at the entrance was long, super bright, and the floor was slick. The walls were white, the floor was white, and the ceiling was white. And I couldn't see one speck of dirt!

"He must have a good cleaner," Bella said. "This place is spotless."

Gently, we closed the door behind us and walked down the hall, which led to a spiral staircase, which was also white.

"We should go up there." I was cautious as I walked through The Collector's home. "That must lead to the area where he's kept all our things."

Slowly, we started up the stairs. Round and round and round and round, we went. There were so many stairs!

"You would think, puff, that, puff, everyone in the future, puff, would have elevators." Tim said, as he struggled up the stairs. "Why so many stairs?"

"Shhh…" I held my index finger to my lip as we reached the top of the stairs. "We don't know what's up here."

I led my friends to the top of the staircase, and we came to another door. I pushed open the door, which led into another large hallway. This hallway was wide enough to be a basketball court, and had lots of closed doors leading off the walls.

"What's that?" Bella asked.

"I think it's a cleaning robot." I whispered as a small round object with arms zipped past us. "It's harmless."

"How do you know that?"

"My dad has talked about them. He's saw them when he went to the future, and Mom keeps asking him to bring one back."

There were around ten robots zipping over the room, cleaning everything as they went. And it wasn't just the robots that were working—there were self-cleaning windows, other robot servants, and a robotic mop. I bet Mom would love that. Maybe I should bring one back for her birthday?

On the wall near the top of the stairs was a large control panel with so many different buttons. I wanted to press all the buttons to find out what they did!

Particularly, the big red button that said 'Don't Touch.' I really wanted to touch that one.

I went to reach for the button, but Tim stopped me.

"No, Jett! We don't know what that button does. Leave it alone. We have to be quiet in here." He pulled my arm back. "Let's keep walking through the house and see if we can find our stuff."

"Oh alright," I moaned.

Quietly, we walked past all the cleaning gadgets, coming closer to one of the strange looking doors.

"What's in there?" Bella asked. "Could that be our stuff?"

We stopped at a door with the number '1640' written on it. Although everything in the house was super modern, this door looked like it was five hundred years old. It was made of dark brown wood, and had a large golden door handle.

"This looks out of place," I said. "Something has to be behind that door. Let's look inside."

"It's probably nothing. Yep, definitely nothing. Totally nothing. Not a thing. Nothing that would interest us. Nope. We shouldn't touch it," Tim replied. "Let's forget about all this and just go home."

But I didn't listen to him.

I reached for the golden handle and twisted it.

"I can't move it," I said as I tried to pull it open. "It's too heavy."

Bella and Tim also tried to pull on the door, and eventually, it started to move. It made a large creaking sound as it opened.

"Whoa." My mouth dropped open once I looked inside the room. "This is amazing!"

Behind the door was a gallery filled with lots of items from the 1640s!

There was a suit of Knight's armor near the door, a display cabinet filled with twenty different swords to the left, and even a horse in the corner of the room!

Bella walked up to the horse and patted it. It neighed loudly, so Bella fed the horse an apple that was sitting nearby.

Tim and I walked around the room, checking out all the stuff from the 1640s.

This was so cool!

"Wow, this stuff is awesome!" I shouted. "This must be The Collector's collection of collected things! I would love to have a room like this!"

"You really shouldn't be touching any of it," Tim said. "It's all very old and wouldn't be any good to anyone. And it probably has all sorts of old diseases on it. You really shouldn't touch it."

"But check out how heavy this sword is!" I picked up a sword that was leaning against one of the knight's armor suits. "This is brilliant! I love this stuff!"

The sword was almost as big as me, but it felt so good to hold.

"Oh, this dress is *so* cool. I wish I could wear something like this to school." Bella picked up a dress from one of the displays. "It's so retro."

"C'mon, this isn't playtime. We're not here to play with all this stuff. The Collector could come back any minute, and if he finds us here, we're toast," Tim complained. "Let's find the stuff that's ours and get out of here."

"He's right," I agreed as I put the sword back. "The Collector could be coming back any second. We have to hurry."

Bella waved goodbye to the horse, and we walked out of the room, pushing the door closed behind us.

"The Collector must be taking all the things from each year and placing it in a room with a matching number," Bella said. "All we have to do is find the room with our year on it. Then we'll find all our stuff!"

"That's perfect!" I yelled. "Let's go! Let's find that room!"

The next door in the hallway had the number '2545' above the door.

"Wow." I stopped. "Let's check this out!"

"No," Tim grabbed my arm. "As cool as that is, we don't have time to find out what's back there. We have to keep moving and find our room before The Collector comes back!"

I really wanted to see what was behind the door with '2545' written on it, but I knew Tim was right. We had to get out of here before The Collector found us!

In a hurry, we ran around the huge building looking for the door with our year on it.

But there were so many doors!

All the doors were from different eras and they were all shaped differently! I would've loved to have looked in each room.

This place was like an amazing museum of the past in the future!

We should do our school trips here. That would be better than going to the park to draw rocks.

"Yes!" I shouted when I found the room with our year written on it. "It's here! I've found our year! Over here!"

Excitedly, Tim and Bella ran over to the door that was shaped like the entrance to an elevator. Tim tapped some buttons on the side panel and then the door made a noise—Ding!

The doors slid open and we stepped inside. It was another large gallery room!

"How awesome is this place!" I said as we walked inside.

Tim and Bella followed me into the room, and right away, we could see all our stuff on display. There was Mr. I. Hurtu's wig, Mr. Chicken's cow, Tim's history book…

And Bella's pig in a pig pen at the back of the room!

"Chris P. Bacon!" Bella ran over and hugged her pig. "I've missed you!"

I searched all over the room but I couldn't find what I was looking for. I looked inside a large cupboard, in the display cabinets, and under the shelves.

"Where is it?" I started to panic. "It's got to be here somewhere."

And then I saw it—Mom's apron!

"Alright!" I yelled as I grabbed it. "Yes! We've got it! Let's get out of here!"

But as soon as I grabbed the apron…**WHACK!**

I was hit from behind!

Hard.

When I looked up, I saw The Collector standing behind Tim and Bella.

And he was pointing a gun at them!

"If you move, your friends will be vaporized!" The Collector laughed, although I didn't find it funny. "It seems not only are you in the wrong place, but you are also in the wrong time!"

Oh man.

This was bad.

Really bad.

CHAPTER 10

We were totally wrecked.

The Collector took us back to the gallery room from our time, and pushed us into the corner. While still pointing his zappy laser gun at us, he put a black box on the ground next to a large lever, pushed some buttons on the box, and then pulled the lever. Suddenly, there were six red laser rings circling around us!

"What's this?" Bella asked as the rings buzzed.

"It's a laser prison. If you touch one of those lasers, you'll be vaporized!" He laughed. Again, I didn't think it was funny.

"What are you going to do with us?"

"You'll make quite the collector's item for my public display." The Collector rubbed his chin. "I'll keep you in this prison forever, and people from my time, which is your future, will look at you like animals in a zoo. You're the ultimate collector's item!"

The rings whirled around us, making a humming noise, and we couldn't do anything!

This was bad as.

I really hoped we didn't have to stay here forever. I could imagine getting quite bored sitting here.

The Collector walked over to the wall near the door, rubbed his fingers against it, and opened one of the metal panes. Behind the pane was a large computer screen, probably large enough to be a cinema screen. The Collector started tapping buttons on the screen and all sorts of pictures appeared. He was documenting all his latest stolen goods, including my Mom's apron, Bella's pet pig, and the three of us.

"Hey Collector, you're so snatched," Bella called out to him. "Totally snatched."

"Kid, I don't even know what that means," he replied.

"LOL. It means I think that you're cool," Bella smiled. "I only came here because my FOMO was through the roof when we were looking at your time machine."

"Are we even speaking the same language?" The Collector sounded grumpy. "What is LOL, or FOMO?"

"Laugh Out Loud, and Fear of Missing Out," Bella called back. "I can teach you more cool things if you let me out."

"No way," The Collector said. "I'm not falling for that trick."

"Bella, what are you doing?" I whispered to her.

"I know that he's a total creeper, but we've got to find a way out of here. We can't spend the rest of our lives in a laser prison in the future. I was just trying to be nice to him to see if he will let us out."

"I don't think that's going to work," I shook my head. "Despite my earlier assumption, I don't think he's friendly."

"Have you got a better idea?"

"Sure," I paused for a moment, and then called out to The Collector. "Hey! Collector! How do we defeat you?"

Bella shook her head and groaned. I don't think she liked my approach.

"You cannot defeat me. I'm unbeatable," The Collector laughed. "I'm the ultimate criminal, and I will never be beaten. I will not be stopped on my quest to collect things from every year."

"You must have at least one weakness," Bella replied. "Everybody has at least one weakness."

"I have one weakness… but you will never figure that out. And I will never tell you. Now, be quiet. I'm trying to concentrate on documenting my newest collector items for my collection of collecting things for the purpose of collection, including three children from your year."

I didn't like that idea.

The future looked cool, but I wasn't keen on spending the rest of my life in a laser prison, being stared at by people who came to look at The Collector's gallery.

"I know." Bella looked around, and whispered into my ear. "I can see a way to escape out of this laser prison, but if I do The Collector will see me. We need to figure out a way to distract him; then I can get us all out."

"But how?"

"Every fifth turn of the laser circles, there's a small gap that I can jump through. I know I can do it, but we have to distract The Collector first."

"He doesn't look like he's easily distracted. He looks like he's a super focused type of guy," Tim added. "That's not going to be easy."

"Let me try a few things," I said. "I'll try to distract him, and you tell me if it works."

I began acting like a monkey to see if it would distract The Collector. I jumped around the laser prison beating my chest and making monkey noises.

Nope. It didn't work.

Bella shook her head again. She wasn't impressed.

I tried playing dead to see if that would distract him.

Nope.

I tried singing.

Still nope.

Yelling.

Nothing.

Dancing.

Nope.

Acting like a bird.

Definitely not.

"Nothing will distract him," Bella whispered. "He's too focused."

"Maybe we just wait until he becomes distracted?" Tim said. "Surely, he can't be focused forever."

So we waited.

And we waited.

And we waited.

But The Collector didn't become unfocused. He sat at his desk for hours, and hours, and hours!

And the prison was *sooo* boring.

Eventually, I had to do something.

I decided to tell some more great jokes to pass the time.

"Hey Tim, have you ever tried to eat a clock?"

"No," Tim looked confused. "Why would I do that?"

"You shouldn't try. It's so time consuming! Ha!"

Tim didn't respond. Maybe he didn't hear me properly. I'll tell him another joke.

"I tried to make a belt out of watches, but it didn't work. That was a... 'waist' of time! Get it! Because the watches go around your waist as a belt, and the watches tell the time! Ha!"

The Collector said something, and Bella was watching him closely.

"Jett, tell another one of your bad jokes," she said.

"Bad jokes? I don't know any bad jokes."

"Alright, alright. Tell another one of your 'awesome' jokes. Just hurry up!"

"What do you call a fast zombie? A zoom-bie! Haha!"

"Agghhh!" The Collector shouted, and he grabbed his head with both hands. "I can't resist it!"

"Jett! Tell another one of your jokes!" Bella said. "Quick!"

"Do you know why there are no card games in Africa? It's because there are too many cheetahs! Hahahaha!"

"Argghhh!" The Collector screamed again! "Stop it!"

"Another one Jett!" Bella yelled. "Hurry!"

"I intend to live forever. So far I'm doing it perfectly!"

"Hahahaha!" The Collector shrieked as he fell to the floor.

"His weakness is bad jokes!" Bella yelled. "Quick Jett! Another one!"

"What sort of clothes does a house wear? A-dress! Haha!"

"Stop it, stop it!" The Collector laughed, doubled over. "I can't take it!"

"They sent me home from school on pajama day. It wasn't my fault; I just sleep naked!"

"Stop! Stop!" he laughed. "It's too much!"

"Why did the picture have to go to prison? Because it was framed! Haha!"

"I'll do anything! Just make it stop!"

The Collector couldn't take bad jokes! That was his weakness!

As The Collector was distracted by my awesome jokes, Bella leapt through one of the gaps in the laser prison and escaped!

She rolled onto the floor, grabbed a skateboard off one of the displays and raced back towards The Collector!

She hit The Collector around the back of the legs while he was laughing, and as soon as The Collector was taken down, Bella hit the lever to turn off the laser prison!

"Sorry, not sorry!" she shouted to The Collector.

Yes!

We were free!

The Collector was lying on the floor laughing, unable to move. He was holding onto his stomach, and he looked like he was in pain from laughing so hard. Not even I thought my jokes were that funny.

"Quick! Go!" Bella yelled. "Move!"

We ran out of the room in a rush—but then we were back into the massive hallway!

Oh no!

"Does anyone remember which door we entered through?" Tim asked. "It all looks the same!"

"Um, nope," I shook my head. "It could be any of them!"

CHAPTER 11

We were back in the hallway of the massive house with no idea how to get out! And the jokes weren't going to keep The Collector down for long! We had to get out of there!

"Check all the doors!" Bella yelled, and opened the door next to her. "Quick! We have to get out of here before The Collector gets us!"

Looking for a way out of the building, we started opening all the doors! Uh-oh. All the doors lead to The Collector's collection of collected things!

This could be dangerous!

There were some very frightening collections here!

There were doors leading to cavemen, ninjas, and cowboys! We had to be careful!

But then… Ah!

Tim opened the door to the dinosaur era!

No!

"Come back!" The Collector ran out of the room from our time. "Get back here!"

Oh no!

He was coming right for us!

I opened another door.

Nope! That was not the exit.

Another door.

Nope!

"Stop!" The Collector yelled. "You're letting out my collection of collected things! Stop it! Come back to me!"

Suddenly, The Collector was right next to me.

In a panic, I jumped through the next door!

But it was a room for the old knight days!

No!

I tried to hide behind an old horse and cart, but The Collector burst through the door, grabbed a horse and a jousting stick, and came charging at me!

Ah! He looked furious!

My great jokes weren't going to work now!

Grabbing the nearest thing to me—a shield and a spiky ball weapon—I charged at him, ready to defend myself!

WHACK!

No!

The Collector hit me with his jousting stick, and it sent me flying out the door into the hallway!

Ouch!

The future totally hurts!

I landed next to Tim, and he helped me up. But just as I got up, The Collector stepped out of the room, and he was right next to us!

And he was mad!

We were doomed!

"Dino…" Tim whispered. "Dinosaur."

"What?" I said.

"Dinosaur!"

"Hide!" I grabbed Tim, and we hid behind one of the doors just as a massive Tyrannous Rex came charging around the corner!

The Collector looked up!

SLAM!

The Collector was knocked into the air!

Yes!

CRUNCH!

The T-Rex hit him again—and he was thrown back into the air!

Looking around the room that we were next to, I saw that it was from the Egyptian times. Grabbing a Mummy sarcophagus tomb, I dragged it out into the hallway.

And…

POW!

The Collector fell straight into the sarcophagus tomb, and the door shut on him! The tomb had a lock on the door—and I locked it shut!

He was trapped inside!

Woo!

The Collector had been collected!

CHAPTER 12

After the dinosaur had walked away, I found Bella hiding in another room.

"I've found our room again," she said. "It's over here. And all our stuff is still in there."

In a hurry, Bella and I collected all the things that had been stolen from our time. I found Mom's lasagna apron, Mr. I. Hurtu's wig, Bella's pig, Tim's history book, and my dad's trumpet.

Strange. I didn't even realize that my dad's trumpet was missing. But he's really, really bad at playing the trumpet, so maybe I'll just leave that there…

As Bella and I finished grabbing all the stolen items, we realized that we hadn't seen Tim for a while.

"Where's Tim?" I asked. "He's not in this room. Where is he?"

"I thought he was with you. I don't know where he is," Bella looked around the large room. "I have no idea where he's gone."

"Oh no. I hope he hasn't gotten himself into more trouble!" I said, and ran out of the room. "Tim?!"

But then we found him standing in the hallway.

"Tim, what have you been doing?" Bella questioned. "And what are you wearing?"

"I've been gathering the clothes from different years for my new fashion look. I love it. I feel really great in these clothes. I think they match my personality perfectly. And they really bring out the color of my eyes. What do you think?"

"Um…" I said.

"I can't even…" Bella shook her head. "I don't even know where to start."

"Yep. I know. I know. It's pretty hard to describe fashion this amazing," Tim smiled. "I should be a fashion designer. People would love to buy clothes like this. I could be an inspiration to millions of people."

I had no idea what he was wearing. All I know was that it looked ridiculous.

"Let's leave all those clothes here, Tim," Bella said calmly. "They're not our clothes. Those clothes were stolen by The Collector, and somebody might actually want them back. Although, I don't know why they would…"

"Oh, alright," Tim sighed and put all his new clothes back. "I wouldn't like to be a fashion designer anyway. Too much pressure."

When we had gathered all the things from our time, we transported them back to the present day using the time machine.

The time machine was really simple to operate; there were only three command buttons: Go, Return, and a place where you enter the Date. No wonder my dad was a top spy, even he could operate one of these things.

It was really fun traveling through time in the machine. It was like a short, fun rollercoaster that didn't scare you. Everyone should try it once. Maybe I could start charging people for rides to the future? Now that would be a great ride at a theme park.

After we had sent all the stolen items back to our time, we grabbed The Collector. He was still locked up in the Mummy sarcophagus tomb, and we could hear him mumbling as we picked him up.

Bella, Tim, the sarcophagus tomb, and I all squeezed into the time machine for one final trip back to the present time. When we arrived, Dad was waiting for us in Dark Park.

"Jett! Bella! Tim!" he yelled as we arrive. "Where have you come from? Have you just traveled through time?!"

"Yes, Dad!" I explained. "We found The Collector stealing all our stuff, so we jumped onto his time machine, and traveled to the future. When we got there, we captured him, got all our stuff, and brought it back with us."

"What?! You shouldn't be traveling through time without years of training from the TTSA! Why didn't you tell me that a time traveling thief was stealing all our things?" Dad said.

"Um, we tried to," I smiled. "But how did you find us in Dark Park?"

"I finally figured out how to use the Exact Location Radar. It told me where the time traveler was landing, and it led me to this location. But when I arrived there was nobody here. Just all this stuff. I figured the thief must have been storing it here and traveling through time. So I decided to wait for them to return. And then you arrived!"

"All this stuff was taken to the future," Bella explained. "The Collector has a large house full of rooms where he stores all the things he has stolen from each year through history. We found the room with our year on it, and all our stolen stuff was inside."

"Except your trumpet, Dad," I added. "We couldn't find that anywhere."

"Oh, ok," Dad looked disappointed. "I miss that trumpet."

"Maybe you could return all the lost items to their proper years?" Bella added. "There was a lot of stuff there."

"Of course," Dad said. "And where is The Collector now? Still causing trouble throughout time?"

"Dad," I smiled. "I have a gift for you."

"A lift? Why would I want a lift?"

"No, Dad. A gift."

"Oh, a gift. Why didn't you say that?"

I really should've bought him a hearing aid, not The Collector.

"Bring him out!" I shouted to Tim and Bella.

They opened up the sarcophagus tomb, and we carried The Collector over to Dad. Dad's eyes almost popped out of his head.

"The Collector!" Dad shouted. "We've been trying to catch him for years! All sorts of years too—from the dark ages through to the future! He has committed so many crimes that he's going to prison for a very, very long time."

"Yes," I said. "That's good news."

"I'm impressed, son. He's the most elusive criminal of all time, and you caught him!" Dad said proudly. "And you've got all our things back! Wow, Jett. You and your friends are amazing."

"But most importantly, I've got Mom's apron back," I grinned. "We can have lasagna again!"

"Ah, good. That's wonderful news, son! Since the apron has gone missing, it's made your mother realize how valuable her lasagnas are. She decided that if the apron were returned, she would go into business. She wants to make a lasagna empire. But she couldn't do it without that apron."

"That's a very good idea," Bella winked. "Who knows what happens in the future?"

Dad stopped for a few moments and put his finger on his chin. "Son, you've proven yourself worthy to be considered for the ultimate honor."

"Really?"

"Yes, son. I've known for a long time that you had the potential to do what's required to become a great Time Spy. After your performance of traveling through time and capturing The Collector, I must consider you ready for the next step. Jetterson Jeffery John James Joseph Baguette, are you ready to become a Time Spy?"

"Yes, Dad. Yes, I am."

"Every Time Spy needs a Time Traveling Watch. This watch protects your body against the rigors of time travel. It automatically adjusts wherever you land. Jett, welcome. You're now a Time Spy."

"Whoa! That's so cool! And I get a Time Traveling Watch!"

"Tim and Bella, you've also proved that you're capable of time travel. I would like to extend the same honor to you, and offer you the chance to train in our agency to become spies of the past, present, and future."

"Cool!" Tim and Bella said together.

"Now, it's really important that nothing traveled from the future back to our time. We do not want anything out of place or time. If that happened, it could have nasty consequences for the future. Are you sure that you only collected the stolen items from our time, and nothing came back from the future, Jett?"

"Absolutely. Not a thing came back with us. We made sure of it."

But just as I said that, I saw Tim and Bella looking at the street behind us…

Oops.

THE END

Printed in Poland
by Amazon Fulfillment
Poland Sp. z o.o., Wrocław

62109577R00070